To our children –
May you go within and discover the courage
to embrace your destiny.

This book is a gift to:

_____

Author's Note

WolfStar is an original fictional tale written in the spirit of and with respect for Native American values and the oral tradition. It is not derived from any particular indigenous North American tradition.

Book Design By John Thompson. The illustrations in this book were hand created using chalk pastels.

This book may be purchased from your local bookstore or directly from the publisher: WolfStar Press, P.O. Box 11168, Boulder, Colorado 80301, (303) 682-1676.

WolfStar
Press

First Printing

ISBN 0-9656422-8-3

Library of Congress Catalog Card Number 97-090058

Printed in Hong Kong

WolfStar

Speak your truth always with courage & compassion.

Donna Chimera

Written By Donna Chimera   **Paintings By Gregg Lauer**

*O*ne cold, quiet night when the moon was full and its silvery light cast mysterious shadows, the woman-child named Snowdeer found herself sitting in a frost-covered field near her village. She touched the hard ground beneath her and saw her breath frozen in the night air as proof that she was not dreaming. Yet, she did not know how she had come to be in this spot. She felt the power of her sister moon move through her and fill her being with a strengthening light that spoke to a source deep within her.

Snowdeer blinked her eyes and gasped as the shadows shifted into the shape of a great silver wolf who beheld her calmly.

"Do not be frightened. The Great Spirit has stirred within you and brought you here to acknowledge that which is soon to be. Your purpose in this turn of the medicine wheel is a noble one. You are to be a new voice, one that speaks for the sisters of the tribe. Too long silent, the gentle and peace seeking voice of the she has been lost in the thunderous rumble of your brothers who seek resolution through competition and aggression against your neighbors. Once a great people, yours has become a warrior tribe. If your people are to survive the generations of storm that are developing, they must set aside their weapons and smoke the pipe of peace, living in harmony with their neighbors and animal friends. To love and respect those with whom they walk this land, this is the sacred path. It is the way of the great mother."

"But I am only a child and a girl child. I have no voice. I have no identity. They will not listen to me," Snowdeer answered timidly.

"Do not fear little one. I am WolfStar, sent to you by the Ancient Ones. I am with you my beloved. I am with you always and will shield you from those who do not yet recognize your destiny. Tomorrow, you are to go to the great lodge and ask to sit among the brothers. This is a time for them to listen. For in your voice is not only the gentle wisdom of the "she" but also the innocent knowing of a child. You may be mocked and jeered, but fear not. Accept the challenges they will set before you. They seek to make you prove that you are worthy. I tell you now—you were born worthy. Upon your successful completion of these challenges, you will be allowed a full and respected voice in the circle of elders.

Go now and sleep upon this night. Tomorrow, before all others arise, go down to the river and cleanse yourself. Wash away all fear and uncertainty and know that you are to be a great voice among your people and all people who will someday inhabit this land you claim as home. After facing the council, go into the forest and speak to your forest allies. Accept what they have to offer you. Judge not whether the gift is worthy of your attention, for indeed, each is blessed by the great mother and will serve you well to meet the challenges which will be set before you."

Snowdeer blinked again and the great wolf was gone.

She returned to her lodge and slipped beneath the skins whose warmth was raised by the sisters who slept with her. She lay there quietly, half hoping that what she had experienced was a dream. Although she found comfort in the gentle snoring of her sisters and the rustling noises of her mother, she missed her father who had left earlier that day with a small hunting party. Her father would know what to do. He did not treat her like her senseless sisters. Rather, he taught her the many things a father would teach his son.

Under her father's guidance, Snowdeer had become a skilled marksman with her bow. She listened carefully to her father as he taught her the ways of the beasts. He taught her a deep respect for mother earth and all her creatures. She was taught to begin each hunt with a prayer of gratitude to the creature that would offer its life to feed its human brothers.

Her people were hungry and she knew that her father was concerned about the increasing discussions about neighboring tribes who were feared to be infringing upon their hunting ground. He maintained a voice of quiet reason and continued to try to calm his more suspicious brothers. Snowdeer knew that her father's hunting party was in truth a scouting party that was trying to determine the intentions of their neighbors.

She climbed out of her coverings and joined her mother, laying at her side as would her father if he were there. She fell asleep breathing in the musky scent of her father which clung reassuringly to the warm skins that covered them.

It seemed she had just closed her eyes when a bright beam of morning's first light broke through a hole in the skins. The light pierced through her forehead and seemed to move through her entire body, warming her to her soul and reminding her of the day's task. While her family still slept, she wrapped a skin around her and slipped out into the quiet sleeping village. She looked with puzzlement at the sky for the sun had not yet risen and she questioned the source of the light that had awakened her from her slumber.

Snowdeer walked down to the icy river and stood on the bank, hesitating to emerge herself. Once again she felt a shaft of light move through her that warmed her to the core of her being. She took a deep breath and dove into the river. The icy water startled her and made it difficult for her to catch her breath. Her limbs numbed and would not respond as she felt herself sinking to the river's bottom. Disoriented in the icy wet darkness, the frightened girl flailed her arms and struggled to find her way back to the surface.

"What is all this commotion so early in the morning?" asked a tiny voice. "Release your fear little sister and open your eyes." Snowdeer forced open her eyes and met the curious gaze of an otter swimming beside her.

4

"Relax." He smiled. "Relax into the knowing that all is well with you. See—there is the morning sun. How could you expect to see the light with your eyes squeezed tight?"

Calmed by the presence of the friendly creature, Snowdeer saw sunlight dancing on the waves above her and she glided upward through the icy water.

Otter splashed along side her and laughed. "And now allow, allow yourself to become the river."

As her body numbed, Snowdeer no longer felt her body as itself. The numbness seemed to strip her of her physicalness and she felt herself as the river, of the river. She relaxed into the beingness of the river, rising and flowing smoothly as the current. The water no longer felt cold, no longer felt foreign; she was the river. She dipped and dove and rose again as did the playful otter. He taught her to move with the flow of the river and to understand that it was the life blood of the land—another expression of the Great Mystery. She felt the greatest sense of peace and belonging that she had felt since she had left the comforting ocean currents of her mother's womb.

Snowdeer heard the noises of her awakening village and began to sense her physicalness once again. Otter splashed her one last time and she laughed with wonder as the water droplets formed into three smooth stones in her hands. Clasping the stones tightly, she swam to shore, dressed and walked slowly to her family's lodge.

The villagers pointed at her and jeered her as a loony one, for the river was thickening with ice and this one was swimming! Her sisters frowned at Snowdeer in embarrassment as her mother wrapped her in warm skins and combed her long tangled hair in front of the fire. Her mother did not scold Snowdeer. Rather, she looked at her daughter deeply and with wonder.

There was a shine to Snowdeer's hair and a glow to her skin that prompted her mother to say, "Daughter, you are less a child every day. I smell in your hair the female current and I feel your heart beating in the rhythm of the great mother. I do not understand why you chose to swim in the icy river, but I think now that it is not necessary for me to understand but to be proud and know that you had a reason, a choice and that you chose to follow the voice within. I have great love for you, my little one."

Snowdeer helped her mother with the daily chores but her mind was not on the grinding of corn or the baking of corn cakes. She was trying to make sense of what WolfStar had told her. Why had she been chosen for such a task? For thirteen years she had been the quiet and largely unnoticed daughter of One Moon and Red Bear. While her two older sisters were considered great beauties and chattered endlessly about the many young braves who sought their attention, Snowdeer preferred to spend her time in the forest or down by the river. She felt more at home with her animal friends than her own people. Surely there was one wiser and more worthy than she to do the bidding of the Ancient Ones.

Snowdeer Speaks

*T*hat evening, as dark clouds passed over the moon, Snowdeer slipped unnoticed into the great lodge. Huddled in a far corner, she listened to the angry words of those who followed the way of the warrior. Gathering her courage, she worked her way between the thick legs of the braves. Moving and blending with the shifting shadows, she found herself standing in front of the old grandfathers—the oldest and most respected voices of the council. When she stepped into the light of the fire, she was met with condescension and anger for daring to interrupt a council on war.

Her small voice was at first lost in the rumbling bravado of the warriors. The great warrior Thundering Elk, youngest of the chiefs, roared with laughter as she asked to speak. Mockingly he said, "Quiet. Let us humor her and ourselves for a moment. For indeed the seriousness of this night's discussion finds welcome the opportunity to laugh. The foolishness of this little one's actions does not discount her courage in entering the lodge to present herself."

Seemingly surprised at his own words, Thundering Elk made a deep mocking bow towards Snowdeer gesturing for her to speak.

Snowdeer began in a trembling voice, "Honored Brothers. I know that I am small and of young voice. But a teacher from the Great Spirit has presented himself to me and instructed me to speak to you. I request to sit among you at the council fire. I do not offer a loud voice but I speak with the clarity of the spirit and always in truth."

Her voice growing stronger, Snowdeer continued, "The history of our land is changing. In near generations, new peoples will blow in with a mighty wind from the east. That wind will blow cold and harsh into the lives of our children and our children's children. It is important now that we seek and enjoy the peace that is still within our reach. We must build strong alliances with our neighboring tribes and instill in our children's hearts the way of peace as the true way for the survival of our people. This wind that comes is inevitable for we must remember that the source of that wind is the breath of the Great Spirit. We can only respect and trust and flow in the currents of change that ride on that wind. That is why we must instill in our children patience and a strong sense of self. They must be prepared to weather the generations of storm and rise again from the settled dust to see clearly what path they must take to return their people to a new and lasting peace within themselves and among the rainbow of peoples that will surround them. Our people will fight to protect the land which they believe to be ours, but in truth we cannot own what is not ours to possess. Battles will be fought and some won. But they will be false victories. For at our heart's core there is no separation, we are one. Fear is our only true enemy."

While many of the braves ignored her or mocked her, those who were closest to Snowdeer heard her words and felt a presence about her. They remembered stories of their ancestor's ancestors who lived in a time when there was peace among the tribes and they had a deep longing in their hearts for that time to return. Thundering Elk was one of these. Though young in years, there was an ancient voice within him that bade him listen, "My son, there is another way . . ." and old memories stirred.

But his pride would not allow him to set his bravado aside. "You seek, little one, to join us at the Council fire. Your words are fervent but they are the foolish dreams of one who has barely left her mother's lap. You have not yet faced this world which you claim is at risk. You have not met its challenges to prove that you are worthy to speak among us."

Thundering Elk was interrupted by one of the Old Grandfathers who said, "Brothers. It is apparent that the little one believes in her story. Let us humor ourselves further and see how strongly she believes in this tale."

With a puzzled look, Thundering Elk turned to meet with other leaders of the tribe. The deep murmuring voices hung heavy and formless in the air like the smoke from the center fire. And the circle of men waited in restless silence.

Finally the Old One spoke in a solemn voice, "There is a disturbing wisdom in the words of this child. But these are disturbing times and we feel it is not wise to ignore the possibility that there is some seed of truth in her tale. Therefore, we have decided that this one known as Snowdeer must prove herself worthy to speak her truth and sit among the brothers at the council fires."

His words were met with discontented rumblings, but none dared to challenge the decision of the Old Grandfathers.

"Your first quest is to prove your courage. You are go to the cave of the Angry Bear and bring to us a claw from the roaring one. Secondly, to prove your cunning, you must find the place of the High Eagle and bring back a feather from the great winged one who flies so high, she touches the face of God. Finally, you say you were given these words from a messenger of the Great Spirit. This is a bold and dangerous claim. Therefore, you must prove to us your spiritual worth. If indeed you are a holy one, then we send you to the darkness beyond to retrieve the Sacred Arrowhead from the Liquid Fire."

The mocking laughter of men in the lodge had faded into a deep uneasy silence as the quests set before Snowdeer were revealed. There were few among the brothers who had successfully wrestled and killed a bear to hold the trophy of a razor claw. The wearing of an eagle feather was reserved for those who had performed feats of courage in the heat of battle. The final challenge was indeed an impossible one. For as many years as the grandfathers' grandfathers had lived and the storytellers could remember, the Sacred Arrowhead had remained untouched by human hands.

Gray Dancer's Gift

*T*he quests were designed to be impossible and she knew that the brothers fully expected her to run from the lodge in tears. They would be done with her.

Instead, Snowdeer raised her voice and spoke firmly, "Thank you my brothers for hearing me. You honor me with the opportunity to prove myself to you. I accept your challenges and humbly ask that you allow me one day to prepare myself for the journey. I do not take my responsibility to my people lightly and will require this amount of time to make adequate preparations."

The Old Grandfathers nodded in agreement but warned her that unless she completed the quests, she would not be allowed to return to her tribe. The young girl stood tall and held her head high as she walked toward the opening of the great lodge. The braves stepped back grudgingly and opened a path before her.

Returning home, Snowdeer tossed and turned in a night of restless sleep. Her dreams were filled with hazy images of a roaring bear, the piercing screams of a high flying eagle and tongues of liquid fire that licked out at her, scorching her skin and beckoning her to step into the flames. She remembered opening her heavy eyes and feeling the comforting arms of her mother wrapped securely around her. One Moon gently rocked Snowdeer and lay cool wet rags across her young daughter's feverish face. The cool rags brought a final image of the great WolfStar.

He spoke gently, "Do not fear your Self. Just as you merged as one with the river, you are the earth and the bear, you are the eagle and the wind, you are the arrow and the fire. Do not fear your Self. Love and appreciate these expressions of the same energy from which you emerged."

With a final great shudder, Snowdeer went limp in her mother's arms and fell into a deep sleep.

When the sun rose, her mother prepared a filling morning meal and pretended not to notice as Snowdeer slipped out the door. The young girl moved quickly before her sisters could remind her of the many chores it was their lot to do.

As she entered the forest, Snowdeer looked around her for an animal to appear and speak to her with the same clarity of the great wolf in her dreams. After much waiting, she grew impatient and sat upon a boulder. Still no sign of the forest allies that the great wolf had promised. Mumbling irritatedly to herself, she felt an acorn drop on her head. She rubbed her head and looked up at the tree overhead and saw a squirrel perched precariously on the end of a branch. She watched the squirrel gathering nuts and carrying them back up the tree. More than once the little creature nonchalantly dropped the cracked shells onto Snowdeer's head. The squirrel scampered down the tree once more. This time, rather than digging for nuts, she ran in front of Snowdeer and chattered busily at her. Snowdeer waved her arms impatiently trying to scare the bothersome creature away. The insulted squirrel suddenly hopped onto her rock and snatched the beaded pouch Snowdeer had set beside her. Snowdeer ran after the teasing squirrel to retrieve her pouch. It was a special gift from her grandmother and contained her favorite shells, medicinal herbs and most importantly, the magical river stones that Brother Otter had splashed into her hands.

Angrily chasing the squirrel, Snowdeer tripped and fell over the large gnarled root of a tree. Her foot caught on the upturned root, pulling it from the ground. As she regained her breath, the squirrel returned and dropped the pouch upon the ground next to the upturned root.

Looking at Snowdeer expectantly, the squirrel then turned and scampered back up the tree. Snowdeer finished freeing the root and brushed off the loose dirt and leaves. She admired its graceful shape and decided that it would make a handsome walking stick for her journey.

Snowdeer felt the urge to remove her leggings and walk barefoot upon the earth. The ground was cold and hard but she liked the sound of the leaves crackling beneath her feet. She carefully collected nuts and berries to sustain her on her journey and added them to her beaded pouch. Not knowing what to expect of her journey, she also carefully sought medicinal roots. She was thankful for her twelfth summer when her grandmother spent many long days patiently teaching Snowdeer about the medicinal herbs, roots and plants that offered themselves from the forest. Although Snowdeer was the youngest of the daughters, the old grandmother knew that the child was special and had chosen her to be the receiver of knowledge of the strong medicine. With her grandmother's passing last spring, the villagers had begun to come to Snowdeer for advice on their ailments and injuries. Even at her young age, they recognized that she had an instinctive knowing of the healing properties of nature's gifts.

Tired from her restless night, she decided to rest and placed her blanket roll beneath her head as she lay down upon the forest floor. Mesmerized by the dappled sunlight that danced through the trees, she saw the spirits within them rise and sway in the early winter wind. Snowdeer slept and dreamt of the great silver wolf, requesting that he appear to her and guide her upon her journey. She felt no fear but rather a longing for company and the comfort of his presence.

She opened her eyes expecting to see WolfStar. But in front of her stood Gray Dancer, an old woman who lived in the caves away from the tribe. Thought to be crazy due to her unkept appearance and constant chanting, she was often seen dancing in the moonlight to a melody that no one else could hear.

Snowdeer sat up quickly, frightened at the wild look of this strange one. Chanting words that were strangely familiar but which Snowdeer did not understand, the old woman reached for her hand. Frightened, Snowdeer snatched her hand away. But Gray Dancer was insistent and Snowdeer understood that the old woman was offering her a gift, a haircomb made of a sharpened and strangely carved shell.

"Old woman. Do you not see I have more serious work to do? I am not my sisters. I do not have time for female vanity and pretty hairpieces," she admonished.

Then Snowdeer remembered that WolfStar had told her to accept that which was offered by the creatures of the forest. Indeed, the appearance of this wild one was more of the animal world than of the human. She reached out and accepted the sharp comb, putting it into her pouch. Looking up to thank the old woman and apologize for her abruptness, she was surprised to see that Gray Dancer was gone. Snowdeer curiously followed the old woman's footprints until they faded away into the undefinable prints of a forest creature. Though the elusive prints had disappeared, Snowdeer felt an urging to begin her journey in the direction of Gray Dancer's footsteps.

Hours later, she glanced at the sun and realized that she had come many miles. Looking back, she could no longer see her village and knew that for the first time in her life, she was truly alone.

Cave of the Angry Bear

Snowdeer thought about the frightening beast her people called Great Angry Bear. For many years her people had heard roaring from the far hills and feared the fierce creature who dwelled within the caves. Those who claimed to see him said he only came out at night. Many a young brave had gone into the great one's cave to prove his courage but none had ever come out.

Snowdeer knew the area where the hills housed the Great Angry Bear and walked cautiously as she searched for the entrance to his cave. Startled by a young rabbit who jumped out in front of her, Snowdeer lost her footing and slipped down the side of a hill. A sudden roaring echoed through the sky and even the trees cowered, revealing an opening in the side of a dark mound.

Taking a deep breath, Snowdeer walked slowly into the darkness and let her eyes adjust to the dim light. She smelled rather than saw the great beast. His pungent odor thickened the air and made it difficult for her to breathe. She felt a rush of air as his paw sliced angrily above her. Surprised that his paw swept across empty air rather than striking an intruder, the bear was caught off guard. Towering above Snowdeer, he looked down at the young human beast and growled curiously at her.

"Why do you trespass in my cave and disturb my slumber?" he grumbled.

"Why do you roar so?" Snowdeer softly questioned back in a quivering voice.

"I respect the courage of such a small one and I sense that you are somehow different from the other human beasts," said the bear as he raised his great right limb and showed Snowdeer that his right paw was missing.

"See what humans have done to me? My paw was lost in a hunter's snare and I roar because my back itches. I get angry when I can't scratch the itch," he said testily. "Besides, I have a wonderful roar and it keeps the other creatures fearful of me."

He lowered his voice, "I do not want them to see that I am not whole. Who would fear or respect me if I am only one half of a bear?"

Snowdeer was filled with compassion and gently laughed. "Come here you silly bear. I have a gift for you." Reaching into her pouch, she pulled out the sharp hair comb that was given to her by Gray Dancer.

As she scratched his broad back, the bear asked her again why she had dared to enter his cave. Snowdeer told Angry Bear about the appearance of WolfStar and the quests set before her by the council.

"I know now that I am in the presence of one blessed by the Great Spirit," said the humbled Bear and asked Snowdeer to turn her back to him. He then lumbered over to a dark corner of his cave where Snowdeer heard him digging and scraping at the earthen floor. When he returned, Snowdeer gasped as he raised his left limb showing her the skeleton of his missing right paw.

He spoke gravely, "Brother Wolf is a pathfinder and a great teacher who has returned to guide your people in these changing times. The Ancient Ones are concerned about the path your people are taking. The sound of war drums shake the heavens and so they have sent WolfStar as a messenger of their concern. It is a great honor for the wolf to come to you, little one. You must listen carefully to his teachings for as he was sent to you, so shall you be sent to others to carry a message of peace as the way of survival of your species."

Lumbering toward Snowdeer, he broke off a claw from the skeleton paw and said, "I have never seen a human creature more worthy than you to wear the claw of Great Angry Bear. Therefore, I give you this piece of myself as a gift from my lineage to yours. Its medicine is tenfold because you wear this claw as a gift rather than a trophy. There was no struggle, no deceit. You came to me with courage and compassion rather than deception and a desire to conquer. Your people have much to learn from you."

Snowdeer patted the bear affectionately. "Thank you my friend. Your words have bolstered my courage and strengthened my resolve. I wear your gift with honor. I promise that I shall return to visit you when my tasks are completed to tell you of my adventures and scratch your back. Although my people shall not know your secret and continue to fear you as the Great Angry Bear, I shall call you "Great Paw" for you have been a generous friend to me upon this most important journey."

Great Paw invited Snowdeer to share the shelter of his cave to protect her from the cold night. Though fearful of fire, he scraped together wood scraps for the human one to build a fire to warm herself. They talked of many things that night—of animal beasts and human beasts and the Great Spirit's plan. He watched over the weary child as she entered the Dream Lodge and thanked the Great Spirit for allowing him to be a part of her journey.

When she awoke, Snowdeer was surprised to find that Great Paw was already gone. She followed his tracks down to the river and watched carefully as he skillfully swiped at the water and the mound of fish on the bank grew. He taught Snowdeer this skill, reminding her that she had already learned how to merge with the river. After blessing the fish who had offered themselves as nourishment, Great Paw and Snowdeer ate a filling morning meal. He nodded with pride as she showed him the bracelet she had fashioned from braided rawhide and his magnificent claw.

Snowdeer knew that Great Paw was reluctant to send her on her way but the kind-hearted bear led her to the mouth of his cave and pointed to a narrow path that would lead her to the high cliffs.

"There, where the ragged cliff greets the sky, lives the most magnificent winged one that I have ever seen. Surely this must be the place of the High Eagle where your brothers send you."

"Go now, little one," he said with gruff fondness, "and may the Great Spirit guide your footsteps."

He then let out a magnificent roar, warning the other creatures of the forest that she was under his protection and that she was to pass safely through the woods. Snowdeer turned and waved goodbye to Great Paw. Raising her eyes to the azure sky, she took the first step of the next part of her journey.

Place of the High Eagle

*A*s she walked through the forest toward the high cliffs, Snowdeer's journey was slow for few had traveled so deeply into the forest and the path was overgrown. She kept her eyes lowered for fear she would fall or the path would disappear and she would become hopelessly lost. It seemed that the more fearfully she concentrated on the path, the more elusive it became and her faltering steps kept her continually off balance. Although grateful for her walking stick, tears of frustration rolled down her cheeks as she made little progress. Brief glimpses of the ragged cliffs through the trees taunted her as they seemed to loom ever farther into the distance.

The dense canopy of high trees hid the late afternoon sun. She shivered at the unfamiliar noises in the forest and longed for the comforting warmth and light of her brother sun. When the path seemed to disappear and the density of the forest finally overwhelmed her, Snowdeer stopped and sank down to her knees. She lifted tired eyes and saw a brilliant patch of blue framed by the towering branches. She watched intently as a great bird made graceful circles in the sky.

Snowdeer studied the bird and realized that it offered no resistance to the wind. Rather, it sought and effortlessly glided on the currents of the Great Spirit's breath. She understood her own resistance to the forest and remembered Brother Otter's advice to release her fears.

She lay down upon the forest floor and, like the multi-colored blanket that her beloved grandmother had woven, Snowdeer wrapped the fallen leaves around her. She breathed deeply of the crisp air, filling her lungs. She breathed slowly and rhythmically until she felt her breath rise and fall with the breath of the living forest. And somewhere between the inbreath and outbreath, the restless beauty of the forest quieted and embraced her.

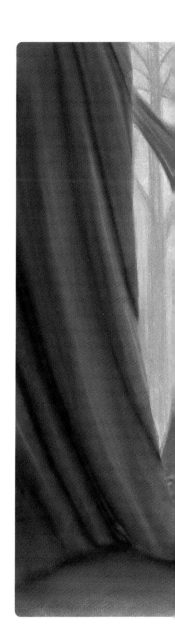

Rested and calmed, she stood up and smiled as the patch of blue grew and the dense brush separated before her. Her feet stepped surely upon the path that whispered, "Here I am. Here have I always been. Trust the Great Spirit and do not let fear be your guide. Lift your eyes up to the sky, lighten your step and let each foot naturally follow the other. The way will always be clear to you."

Time passed quickly as Snowdeer began to notice the squirrels up in the branches, strange birds with new melodies and shy deer as they peeked through the brush. The sun was low in the sky when the path finally led out of the forest.

With the forest behind her, Snowdeer looked in awe at the great ragged cliffs that rose to challenge the sky. The setting sun painted a soft hued canvas which softened the cliffs and made them somehow less forbidding. She found a protected spot at the base of the cliffs, built a fire and sat eating the berries and nuts from her pouch. She said a silent thank you to Great Paw for filling her belly that morning. She then blessed the earth she laid upon and requested a peaceful night in the Dream Lodge to prepare her for the next day's task.

Shivering in the cold night air, she awoke once and found that WolfStar had joined her. She smiled sleepily at him as he came and lay down beside her. Too tired to speak, she snuggled against his warm coat, breathed deeply of his musky scent and fell back to sleep to the even beating of his heart.

When Snowdeer awoke, WolfStar was gone but his familiar scent lingered in the morning air. Although she had hoped for his company this day, she was grateful for his warm presence on the previous night. She looked toward the rising sun and the warmth it too promised. She then bowed her head reverently in the seven directions, asking for their blessings as she began another day. North, south, east, west, earth, sky, and inner . . .

Squinting up at the cliffs that were sharply etched against a blue sky, Snowdeer began her slow ascent up the treacherous rock. The rock that had seemed so beautiful in the setting sun now loomed threateningly above her and its razor sharp edges warned her that this was not a place that welcomed humans. Each step was measured and she was totally focused in the moment. Snowdeer was not thinking of her people, her family or even the reason for her climb. She did not look above her to the unknown heights nor behind her at the depths below. She looked only for the next piece of rock to grasp and lift her upward.

After long hours of climbing, her concentration was broken by the muffled chirping of a frightened bird. Searching for the source of the pitiful cries, she looked down and discovered a fledgling eagle that had fallen from its nest and now sat precariously perched on a piece of broken brush that grew from the side of the harsh rock. She groaned as she realized she would have to retrace her hard won steps down the cliff in order to reach the young bird.

Snowdeer lowered herself as close as possible to the frightened creature but found that it was still beyond her reach. She took her walking stick and saying a silent thank you to the squirrel, she lowered the gnarled tree root down to the frightened creature. Coaxing it on to her walking stick, she reached for the bird and held it gently to her. She promised to return it to its mother and continued her slow, steady climb upward.

As she rose higher, there were fewer and fewer handholds. With each step she extended herself further, searching for the next elusive outcropping to grip. Her breathing became increasingly labored and the altitude was beginning to make her dizzy.

Suddenly a piercing scream filled the sky and Snowdeer looked up to see an enormous bird whose outspread wings shadowed the sun. A great mother eagle swooped down to rescue her child from the human intruder. Frightened by the angry eyes of the approaching bird, Snowdeer lost her balance and began sliding down the rock. Razor edges sliced her knees and vicious bushes cruelly tore at her hair. The mother eagle swooped down again and this time grasped Snowdeer by the neck of her dress, carrying the human child and her own higher and higher to the outcropping of rock that touched the sky. Curiosity overcame her fear and Snowdeer looked with wonder at the land below her. She was amazed at the expanse of land, the generous bodies of water and the many creatures who looked up respectfully as the great bird's shadow passed over them.

The mother eagle landed easily and gently set the children down into the nest. The wings that had spread so menacingly against the sky now wrapped protectively around her son and she stroked him tenderly with her beak. After nuzzling her now safe son and examining him for any harm, she once again turned angry accusing eyes at Snowdeer. The young bird chirped excitedly to his brothers and mother, explaining how he had fallen from the nest when he had attempted flight and that the human beast had rescued him. The mother eagle's eyes softened and she thanked Snowdeer for saving her son.

Snowdeer stared in awe at the majestic bird. Never had she seen such a magnificent creature. Surely this must be the nest of High Eagle.

Acknowledging Snowdeer's thoughts, High Eagle nodded her head and said, "Yes, I am the one your people have named High Eagle. Why have you come to my piece of the Earth? I thought that I had chosen well—that my family was safe from the intruding human beasts. Why do you seek me?"

Snowdeer told High Eagle of her instructions from WolfStar and her appointed quests. "If I bring back a feather from the great winged one, you who touch the face of God, then I will be one step closer to proving that I am worthy to join the council of elders. Even now I fear that I may be away too long. The angry words of war gain momentum with each gathering of my brothers."

The noble bird nodded her head, "I watch the actions of the human beasts with deep sadness. From my place in the sky I see each fearful human gathering. Clouds of angry words darken the sky and mother earth echoes with the increasing vibrations of war drums. Tell your people to release their fears. From the heights I see that there is an abundance of land and food and water. There is enough for all who walk this land. The Great Spirit provides for all creatures in his divine plan, but I fear he grows intolerant of the greed of the human beasts."

Her piercing eyes looked solemnly at Snowdeer, "Little one. Your brothers seek to make you prove you are worthy to sit among them by stealing a piece of myself from me. They are fools. They see my feathers as powerful medicine for they believe that is how I touch the face of God. They have forgotten that there was a time when even your species held the magic of flight. But the gravity of their fear has weighed them down and limited them to walks upon the earth. It has hampered their vision for now they see only that which is directly in front of them and live in fear that there is not enough to provide for all of the Great Mother's children."

Snowdeer's heart pounded in her chest and she listened carefully as High Eagle continued, "I tell you now, little one, that you touch the face of God each time you raise your face to the sun, lift your tongue to taste the rain and sing with the crickets at night. Indeed, the face of God is in your reflection when you cleanse your face in the river. However, I understand that your brothers are still asleep and demand proof of that which cannot be proven—what simply is. Therefore, as a gift, I offer you a feather from my nest. When you are cold, remember the warmth of my nest and you will be warmed. When your belly is empty and your limited vision leads to a fear that there is not enough, remember the abundance you saw as you looked down from the heights. And when the gravity of your people's fears weigh you down, remember who you are. You are a true descendent of those who understood sacred flight and your spirit will soar into the welcoming arms of the Ancient Ones."

Snowdeer bowed her head in gratitude to High Eagle and solemnly accepted the sacred feather. "Thank you, High Eagle. This a great honor you bestow upon me. I shall wear it with integrity and remember the wisdom of the noble one who bestowed it so generously upon me. And now I beg your indulgence and ask your guidance regarding my third and final quest. I know my brothers mock me by sending me to retrieve the Sacred Arrowhead from the Liquid Fire. Although the storytellers have long spoken of this great weapon, we know not where it is. They say it was carved by the Ancient Ones when they still walked the earth and was forged in the fire of original source. It carries the secret of the ages—the secret of our survival. It is said that it will fly swiftly on the breath of the Great Spirit and pierce its every target. They say they have been told that there is one who will come to retrieve the Sacred Arrowhead and is worthy to possess it. We have long waited for a warrior with the skill to use it in protection of our people and believe that those who possess the Sacred Arrowhead will be recognized as most powerful and will have the respect of all others. As keepers of the Sacred Arrowhead, no others will dare to challenge my people's right to claim all they desire. We will not fear hunger again."

High Eagle frowned and shook her head at the earnestness of Snowdeer's speech, "Continue."

42

"Many braves have searched for the arrow and some have even claimed to have found the secret place where it dwells. They say that no mortal man could withstand the heat and flames that spew from the Liquid Fire. My grandmother spoke to me of a time while she still sat on her mother's lap when a hunting party returned bearing the body of a blinded and horribly burned young brave from her tribe. A respected warrior, he had found the place of the Sacred Arrowhead and had even stepped into the flames in an attempt to reach it. He mumbled incoherently that on the arrowhead he had seen strange carvings that seemed to rise up from the stone and have a fiery life of their own. Although he lived, he was blind and so horribly disfigured that none could bare to look upon his face. He left the tribe and wandered in madness, telling his terrible tale to anyone who would listen."

The eaglets had listened wide eyed to the serious discussion of their mother and the curious human child, but now their bellies were empty and they chirped for High Eagle's attention.

"Indeed, I know of the secret place where the Sacred Arrowhead awaits. However, I am not certain this is the time or you are the one chosen to free it from the fires. How could so important a role be given to one so young and innocent? My little ones are hungry now. It is time to fill their bellies. We will talk more of this in the morning after a good night's sleep."

High Eagle told her children to be patient and she would return with their dinner. While she was gone, Snowdeer played with the young birds and laughed as they tried to teach her to fly as their mother was teaching them. The young bird she had rescued sat on the far side of the nest, tired of the teasing he had received from his brothers.

High Eagle returned with pieces of meat that she carefully shredded for her young. Realizing that the raw meat was not to the liking of the human child, she left again and returned with a branch full of berries for Snowdeer. Their bellies full, the young birds nestled close to their mother and chirped lovingly under the protection of her great wings.

Snowdeer smiled sadly and felt homesick for her own pallet in her family's dwelling. She had enjoyed playing with the young birds earlier but was reminded of her own sisters and friends and wondered what they were doing. It seemed so long since she had played the games of a child.

Her muscles ached and the ragged scrapes on her legs stung. She opened her pouch and winced as she squeezed the liquid from a root on to the open wounds. Snowdeer longed for the comforting arms of her own mother and lonely tears rolled down her tired cheeks.

High Eagle expanded her great wings and drew Snowdeer close to her brood, "This is too heavy a burden for one so young to bear. I do not understand why brother WolfStar has chosen such an innocent for so dangerous and wearisome a task. But it is not my place to question the wisdom of the Ancient Ones."

Seeking to comfort the child, High Eagle whispered softly, "Look up to the sky little one. Do you not know that these are the same stars that shine over your mother and sisters? Truly there is no distance between your heart and theirs. Look now to the star that shines directly over your heart for that is where your beloved guide dwells. Look deep into the light of that star and perhaps the great WolfStar will take you to your mother for a nightflight that will ease your lonely heart."

Snowdeer's eyes became heavy as she looked deeply into the intense light of the star over her heart and listened to the gentle crooning of High Eagle. That night she dreamt of WolfStar as he stepped down from the midnight sea of darkness.

"All is well with you child. We are greatly pleased with your progress on this journey. We have chosen carefully and trust that you will not disappoint us. You are very brave for one so young in years. We understand that you are lonely for your mother and we desire to ease your longing. Come now."

Snowdeer climbed upon his broad back and he carried her through the sky to her village. The midnight air should have been cold but the starlight warmed her and she breathed deeply of the black nectar of the night sky. How quiet her village was. It saddened her to think that only in a dream state were her people at peace with themselves and their neighbors.

WolfStar took her through the walls of her lodging and gently laid her down beside her sleeping mother. Snowdeer traced her finger down the tear stained cheek of One Moon and stroked her raven hair. With an imperceptible sigh, her mother stirred slightly and a smile touched her lips. Snowdeer cuddled closer to her mother and finally slept.

Snowdeer was awakened by the hungry chirping of the young eaglets. She looked around for High Eagle but the mother had already flown to find a morning meal for her hungry children. Snowdeer snuggled into the downy feathers that lined the nest and thanked WolfStar for the beautiful nightflight into her mother's arms. She felt rested and refreshed and ready to begin the final quest.

When High Eagle returned, she turned a solemn eye to Snowdeer and said, "I know the place of the Sacred Arrowhead in the Liquid Fire. I too, took a nightflight to meet with the Ancient Ones. They have given permission for me to lead you to the secret place. I now understand that a very old and wise soul resides in this human child known as Snowdeer and I trust the wisdom of the Ancient Ones. They have long awaited your return and I am honored to assist you in your quest."

Snowdeer climbed upon the back of High Eagle and waved goodbye to her noisy, young brood. High Eagle cast a stern but loving eye on yesterday's adventurous son and reminded him that he was not yet ready to spread his wings in flight.

Raising her own mighty wings, High Eagle lifted Snowdeer to greet the morning sky. Snowdeer thrilled at the incredible view of the earth. She was again struck by the abundance of all that the mother offered to meet the needs of both the human and the animal beasts. She studied High Eagle's patterns as she rose and expertly dived to catch the current of the Great Spirit's breath. Memories stirred in Snowdeer as they effortlessly glided on the morning winds and she had a sense of another time, another place, another flight . . .

50

The Final Quest

*W*hen the sun was at midpoint in the sky, High Eagle began her descent to the earth below. Snowdeer looked with apprehension at the landscape below her. Enormous ragged rocks formed a rough circle around an expanse of flame scarred forest. Lifeless charred trees stood eery sentinel over a huge smooth stone that stood in the center and rose out of an angry black pool of liquid fire. There, protected in the heart of the fire, lay the Sacred Arrowhead.

High Eagle gently lowered Snowdeer to the last patch of live earth outside the forbidding circle of blackened stones, "I know this is a frightening place little one, but I can go no further. The time has come for you to fulfill your chosen destiny. Remember you are not alone. With each step you take, the spirits of Brother Otter, Great Paw, High Eagle and WolfStar accompany you. Remember who you are, for indeed it was your choice to return to this turn of the medicine wheel to assist the human family."

Snowdeer clung to the wing of High Eagle, "I'm frightened. I do not understand why you say I chose this burden for myself. I do not know what I am to do, I do not know who I am. Please do not leave me."

With the sad eyes of a mother wanting to protect her child and take her far from the frightening place, High Eagle freed herself from Snowdeer's grasp. As if weighed down with a heavy heart, she slowy rose to the sky, made three protective circular patterns around Snowdeer and then turned back toward home.

Snowdeer sank to the precious grass beneath her and buried her face in the leaves. She treasured the live smell of the leaves and chose a beautifully formed one to place in her pouch. Taking a deep breath, she stepped onto the sooty barren earth in the shadow of the forbidding black circle of rocks that outlined the Sacred Arrowhead's territory.

The circle of rocks cast a chilling shadow. Shivering, Snowdeer looked up to the sky, but even the sun seemed an unwelcome visitor to this dark and lonely place. She passed between two of the boulders and could feel the heat rise from the scorched ground. Ashes covered her boots and floated eerily around her, taunting her and daring her to go further into the sacred place. She understood how the warrior from her grandmother's story had sunk into madness, for indeed, this was a place of madness.

"How could a sacred place be a source of such darkness?" she wondered aloud.

"There is no source of darkness, little one, there is only absence of light. And you, Snowdeer, are the light that will bring this sacred place to life once again," answered WolfStar who, unnoticed, had joined Snowdeer.

"Oh, beloved friend. Thank you for coming to me," Snowdeer said gratefully as she buried her face into his coat.

"I have never left you, my child," he answered softly.

"This place was not always as you see it now. There was a time when it was green and fertile and home to many creatures who respected but held no fear of the liquid fire. They co-existed peacefully and the animals respected the Sacred Arrowhead and its powerful medicine. And then the human beasts heard of the existence of the Sacred Arrowhead and imbued it with a significance born of their ever increasing greed and desire to possess what was not theirs to possess. They decided that to hold the Sacred Arrowhead would assure them victory over those whom they no longer recognized as brothers. Words of anger and hatred and destruction were carried on stronger and stronger winds of fear and separateness. And then one day, those winds were so mighty that they grabbed the flames, dragging them out into the fertile forest. The forest was quickly consumed and many rare and beautiful creatures sacrificed their lives to human fear. To this day, the descendants of those early creatures have a great fear of fire."

"But why would the Great Spirit allow such a horrible event to take place?" asked Snowdeer. "Could he not have sent the rains to stop such destruction?"

"This is a harsh lesson to learn. The Great Spirit allows all things as his creations evolve. He knew that there would come a time when the human beasts would say, 'Enough. We are tired of living in fear. Show us another way.' The Ancient Ones have waited patiently for such a day. They look upon you with great favor, Snowdeer, for they see burning in your heart a desire for peace and they have offered you the honor to raise that same understanding in your angry brothers."

The ground was becoming increasingly hot beneath their feet as Snowdeer and WolfStar walked deeper into the heart of the circle. Tightly clutching the fur around her guide's neck, Snowdeer looked up at the tall barren trees which stood naked in the eerie gray sky. It was not the nakedness of trees in winter who would blossom again in the spring. This was the forlorn nakedness of once living creations who had given up hope of new life and hardened themselves with that realization into petrified stone.

Snowdeer began to feel faint with the heat and she found it increasingly difficult to breathe. Her tongue was swollen and her parched lips were cracked.

She sank to the ground and moaned, "It is too much. I cannot go any further WolfStar. Please forgive me. I have failed you."

"Do not despair little one. Remember your gift from Brother Otter," WolfStar answered.

Snowdeer reached into her pouch and removed the stone droplets which Brother Otter had splashed on her so long ago. Remembering her cleansing plunge into the river, she ran the stones across her face and squeezed cool drops of water into her parched mouth. The river stones were as refreshing as the icy drops of water from which they were formed. She then turned to her beloved WolfStar and shared the last drops of precious water. Together they thanked Brother Otter for his gift.

Refreshed, they continued toward the center—the pool of Liquid Fire. The heat became intolerable and Snowdeer began to sway dizzily in front of the flames. She could see the Sacred Arrowhead positioned in the white hot heart of the fire. Strange carvings rose from the arrowhead and danced tauntingly. She turned to reach for WolfStar but he was gone.

Mesmerized by the flames, she gasped as they molded themselves into the shapes of an otter, a bear, an eagle and a wolf. The flames licked out at her, beckoning her to step into the inferno and reach for her destiny. Had her friends betrayed her? Had they tricked her into coming to this place? Had she slipped into madness?

Snowdeer lifted her eyes and cried, "Great Spirit come to me. Release me from this madness. Bring me home to you."

Snowdeer felt as though she was on fire. Then she realized that the heat was not from the flames outside of her, but from somewhere within her own being. The flame of eternal life, that which burns in each soul, was called to life by Snowdeer's plea. It grew and grew and she felt herself transforming, returning to her original soul form. She looked with wonder at her body as it glowed and flowed into the pool of fire. Ancient sparks from the same sun, she merged with her animal friends and rose with them into the living flames of the Liquid Fire. The once menacing flames now welcomed her, and lifting their gift into the air, offered the Sacred Arrowhead to Snowdeer. She reached fiery arms toward it and grasped it with flaming fingers. Sinking back into the pool surrounding the great stone, she thanked the Great Spirit and felt herself re-emerging into physical form.

Fully awake and aware of her transformation, Snowdeer sensed her body cooling. She felt a great rumbling beneath her as mother earth reached up to reclaim the black liquid pool that had originated deep in her womb. Snowdeer watched the timeless flames, as if weary of burning, sink gratefully back into the earth.

Exhausted from the experience, Snowdeer, too, fell to the earth and slept for a long, long time.

Snowdeer dreamt of crystal flakes of winter's first snow that tickled her eyelashes and wetted her lips. She lay for a moment with her eyes still closed, relishing the cool but tender touch of the flakes on her face.

When she opened her eyes, she was greeted by the welcome face of her beloved WolfStar. The mighty wolf was somehow different. He did not speak to her but nudged her affectionately with his snout urging her to awaken. Snowdeer laughed with pleasure as she realized the snowflakes were real. She sat up and saw that she was surrounded by forest creatures eager to thank the human child for releasing the Sacred Arrowhead and returning the forest to them.

Snowdeer searched the snow for the Sacred Arrowhead and grasped it in her hand. She cried out in brief pain as the Sacred gift branded its message into her palm. The mysterious markings that had been indecipherable on the Arrowhead were now reversed on her hand. Tears of understanding flowed down her cheeks as she read its message. Now, Snowdeer truly understood the powerful medicine of this gift from the Ancient Ones. The sacred truth of the arrowhead was not one of death but of life. It was not a weapon to be raised in war against a brother, but a talisman of peace waiting to be worn around the neck of the one brave enough to grasp it, wise enough to understand it and courageous enough to speak its truth. She took a piece of rawhide from her pouch and tied the Sacred Talisman around her neck.

"Come WolfStar, we must hurry back to my people before it is too late. I pray that the great Spirit has kept them fed so that rumblings of hunger in their stomachs do not lead to the final rumblings of war."

She looked expectantly at the wolf to tell her what she should now do. Though the majestic animal stared at her with loving eyes and stood protectively beside her, he did not respond. Raising her arms to the sky, Snowdeer cried, "Great Spirit ,why have you taken the voice from my beloved WolfStar?"

The skies too were silent. Through contemplation, Snowdeer understood that she had been through the fire, she had merged with her animal friends and their wisdom was instilled in her. There was no longer a need for them to communicate verbally with her. All the knowledge of the heavens and the earth was available to her.

Snowdeer noticed a magnificent stag that stood beyond the animals which encircled her. She walked over to him and said, "Brother, I ask you now to carry me to the village of my people that we may bring the medicine of the Sacred Arrowhead to my human family before it is too late."

The noble beast bowed its head and lowered to its knees, allowing Snowdeer to climb upon his powerful back. She pointed to the sky where a great eagle was circling and said, "Follow High Eagle and she will lead us back to my people."

Snowdeer turned, waved goodbye to the other creatures and smiled at her beloved guide who ran alongside her as she sat astride the mighty stag. Time was immeasurable. They ran like the wind, following the course outlined by High Eagle.

Thundering Elk

*T*he early evening sky was heavy with swirling dark clouds and thunder rumbled as Snowdeer finally looked down from the snow covered hills above her village. Her heart pounded fearfully as she realized that it was not thunder that vibrated in the air, but war drums. Many war drums.

Lifting her eyes and raising her trembling arms to the heavens, she prayed, "Great Spirit, give me the strength of Great Paw, the vision of High Eagle and the wisdom of WolfStar that I might find the way to reach into the hearts of my people and those with whom they prepare to war!"

Snowdeer looked again toward her village and saw that a small band of scouts carrying the colored lance of her people's enemies were hiding in the trees beyond the field where she had first spoken to WolfStar. She pulled a last piece of rawhide from her pouch and wrapped it around her head. She tucked High Eagle's feather firmly into the band, tightened the claw bracelet on her wrist, and gently touched the Sacred Arrowhead to her lips.

Descending the hill, she watched as a group of her own tribe's warriors gathered opposite their enemies on the village side of her field. Searching for her father, instead she recognized Thundering Elk in his war headdress and whispered, "Wait for me, my brother. Are you then so eager to die?"

Thundering Elk raised a puzzled brow as he turned toward the hill that Snowdeer descended. He stared in disbelief at the fast approaching young woman with an eagle feather in her band and a wolf by her side. She sat astride a magnificent stag as naturally as he sat upon his own favorite war horse. When she came closer, he gasped sharply as he saw the Sacred Arrowhead emblazoned on her chest, casting a light that surrounded her. Was this the child they had sent out so long ago?

He felt the same ancient memory that had stirred in him that night in the lodge, "My son, there is another way . . ."

As Thundering Elk turned to instruct his warriors to wait, he realized that their enemies had also seen Snowdeer. They too recognized that this strange child had possession of the Sacred Arrowhead and they wanted it!

"Snowdeer!" he cried as he rode out to her and watched in horror as an enemy warrior raised his bow and took aim at the young woman.

Snowdeer turned in the direction of his enemy and raised her right hand. Other warriors in the band, eager for the glory of possessing the Sacred Arrowhead, ignored her raised hand and released their own deadly arrows. The first arrow struck the stag beneath her and the creature stumbled. The second arrow pierced the side of the great wolf who ran at her side. Thundering Elk swerved in front of Snowdeer to try to protect her but Snowdeer accepted the fate she had chosen. The third arrow pierced the chest of the beautiful woman-child.

Thundering Elk caught Snowdeer as she slipped off the back of the loyal beast.

"What have we done?!" he cried aghast. Blinded by the light of the Sacred Arrowhead, he vowed, "You will be avenged!"

Snowdeer gently shook her head, "My Brother, there is another way." Fingering the Sacred Arrowhead around her neck, she whispered, "I entrust to you the medicine of the Sacred Arrowhead for I know that the memories are stirring and the Ancient Ones will guide you. I came from the Great Mystery and to the Great Mystery I shall return. Do not fear. I shall be with you my Brother." With a final peaceful sigh, she closed her eyes and lowered her head.

A strange glow lit up the darkness and dissipated the clouds above them. A silent tear rolled down the great warrior's cheek as he reached for the Sacred Arrowhead with its unfamiliar markings. He cried out in pain as the Sacred Arrowhead turned red hot and seared its message into his trembling hand.

Thundering Elk climbed upon his own horse and rode into the village with Snowdeer in his arms. His men, victorious over the small band of enemies, rode proudly toward their respected leader. Ignoring them, the grieving warrior rode toward the Great Lodge.

His eyes begging silently for forgiveness, Thundering Elk gently lowered Snowdeer into her father's arms and dismounted.

Loudly vowing to avenge the death of the child, the villagers were eager to see the Sacred Arrowhead and excitedly discussed the power it gave them over their enemies.

"Fools!" roared Thundering Elk. "You understand nothing! We are not worthy of this gift that cost the life of so pure a spirit." With an anguished cry, he hurled the Sacred Arrowhead into the heavens where it burst into a fiery constellation in the winter sky. His people and the enemy warriors raised startled eyes to the heavens and trembled at the fury of the Ancient Ones as the skies flashed and rumbled angrily.

Humbled by this message from the Ancient Ones, wonder overcame their fear. The enemy Chief and remaining warriors rode slowly toward the light that beamed down on Thundering Elk.

Raising his right hand toward the Old Grandfathers, Thundering Elk said solemnly, "My people, hear me. This is the Ancient Ones' message of the Sacred Arrowhead. This is the powerful medicine that will protect our people. This is the truth that will allow our children's children to continue to walk upon this earth . . ."

And the Old One stepped forward to read aloud the message branded upon the hand of Thundering Elk—

"Look into my eyes Beloved mine and behold yourself,
Look into my eyes Enemy mine and behold yourself.
For at the core we are One and
One divided against itself will surely perish."

Women sobbed, warriors lowered their weapons and there was a silent understanding.

Thereafter, Thundering Elk was recognized as the Peacemaker. He set aside his lance and carried instead the pipe of peace. Entering each village with his hand raised in a gesture of peace, he spoke for his tribe and he spoke for humankind. He told the story of brave Snowdeer and shared the wisdom of Brother Otter, Great Paw, High Eagle and WolfStar. The powerful voice that formerly sounded words of war now spoke fervently of the path of peace to be laid down between the tribes.

The storytellers say that the Peacemaker followed the arrowhead constellation in the night sky and when the moon was full, they say, that one who would look closely would see a great silver wolf and a young maiden walking along beside him.

The End